The
Littles
and the Terrible Tiny Kid

by John Peterson
Pictures by Roberta Carter Clark
Cover illustration by Jacqueline Rogers

A
LITTLE APPLE
PAPERBACK

SCHOLASTIC INC.
New York   Toronto   London   Auckland   Sydney

ISBN 0-590-45578-8

22 21   1/0

Printed in the U.S.A.   **40**

First Scholastic printing, April 1993

To Holly Simmonds Peterson,
    my wife, friend, and number-one
    consultant on the Littles,
    without whose help Cousin Dinky Little
    could never have written his songs
    about the Littles' adventures.

IT was a few minutes before twelve noon
on a Saturday. Tom and Lucy Little stood
on the roof of the Biggs' house near the
chimney. They were about to send a message to Tina Small, one of their friends.
Ten-year-old Tom, and his sister, Lucy,
eight, knew that Tina would be standing
on the roof of the house nearest them,
waiting for the message.

Noontime—with the bright sun right
overhead—was Mirror-Message Time in
the Big Valley. Tom and Lucy tilted their
small piece of mirror toward the sun. The
sun reflected off the mirror. The sunlight
from the mirror made a small spot of light
on the Biggs' yard far below them.

When they moved the mirror, the spot
of light moved quickly across the lawn. It

raced through the nearby woods between the two houses.

Now Tom and Lucy could see the light spot on the roof of the house where Tina lived. They pointed it at the chimney where they knew Tina would be standing.

"In a second she'll signal dash-dot-dash," said Tom. "That's a 'k' in Morse code, and it means we should go ahead with our message."

"I *know*, Tom!" said Lucy. "You don't have to tell me every time."

They waited for Tina's signal.

"No answer," said Tom after a few seconds. He wiggled the mirror. "Maybe she'll see this."

There was still no answering flash of light.

"She should be there," said Tom.

Lucy squinted at the chimney of the nearby housetop. "I wish I could see her!" she said. "Darn it! Sometimes I wish we weren't *so* tiny!"

TOM

MR. LITTLE

MRS. LITTLE   BABY BETSY

GRANNY

Tom and Lucy were indeed tiny. All nine members of the Little family were. And they weren't just small—they were teeny tiny. (The biggest Little was just six inches tall.)

UNCLE PETE

The Littles lived in a small ten-room apartment inside the walls of a house owned by Mr. and Mrs. George Bigg and their son, Henry. The Biggs had no idea that tiny people were living in the same house with them. Tina Small and her family also lived in a house with big people. It was that way all over the Big Valley. The tiny people always stayed out of sight, and the big people knew nothing about them.

UNCLE NICK

Were the Littles like big people in any way? Yes, they were, in almost every way except one—the Littles had tails. And they enjoyed having them. They liked the way their tails looked and felt.

GRANDPA

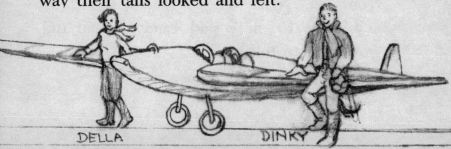

DELLA

DINKY

And, like most people, they had friends to visit. (Not often. The distances between houses were great and traveling was dangerous.) To keep in touch they sent letters by airmail, delivered by Cousin Dinky Little and his wife, Della, in their gliders. And, on sunny days at noon, they flashed mirror-messages to one another across the Big Valley.

Tom and Lucy always looked forward to getting letters or messages from their friends. Now, Tina wasn't answering their signal.

"She isn't there or she'd answer," said Lucy. "She forgot. How could she forget?"

"What did you want to say to her?" Tom asked.

"I wanted to know what she was wearing," said Lucy.

"Lucy! That's not important," said Tom.

"It is to me," said Lucy. "What did you want to tell her?"

"I had a knock-knock joke I wanted to do," Tom said. "I got it from Henry Bigg's joke book."

"Oh, I suppose that's important," said Lucy.

"No," said Tom. Then he laughed. "But it is funny."

Just then a dog began barking loudly in the Biggs' front yard below them. Tom and Lucy looked down and saw the dog running in circles, barking, and leaping up at the base of a tree near the road. Nearby was a parked car and a man changing a tire.

"What's that dog barking at?" said Tom.

"I see what it is!" yelled Lucy. She pointed. "There are two tiny people climbing the tree, trying to get away from the dog."

"Uh-oh!" said Tom. "They're not high enough up the tree."

In a second the tiny boy tilted the mirror downward and sent a beam of reflected sunlight directly into the dog's eyes. The animal stopped jumping and barking at once. It turned its face away from the bright light. Every time the dog turned back toward the tiny people, Tom shined the light in its eyes again. In the meantime the tiny people had climbed up to a tree limb where they were out of the dog's reach. Tom kept on directing the beam of light at the dog's face until the dog went away.

While Tom was chasing away the dog with the mirror, Lucy was looking hard at the tiny people. "They're kids, I think," she announced, "a girl and a boy. And, Tom—from here they don't look like anyone we know."

"Gee—strangers!" said Tom. "I'll flash them a message. I hope they know the Morse code." Then he directed short and long flashes of reflected sunlight toward the children in the tree. He spelled out: STAY THERE. WE'RE COMING.

Tom and Lucy hurried through the secret shingle door in the roof to the attic. From there they got into the tin-can elevator that went to the floors below. It was made from an old soup can and some pieces of string. Tom pulled on one of the strings and the elevator went down to the cellar. Finally, they left the house through a secret door known only to the Littles and their friends.

Tom and Lucy ran across the Biggs' yard to a tree near the road. There they found the two tiny strangers who had just climbed down from the tree limb. One was a girl about Tom's age and the other

was a boy who was younger than Lucy.

"Hello!" said Tom. "I'm glad you escaped from that dog."

"Did you see what happened?" asked the girl.

"Yes!" said Tom and Lucy together.

"We could have gotten up that tree faster but some dope was shining a bright light in our eyes," said the girl. "Crimeny! I could hardly see."

"Oh?" said Tom. He looked at his sister and shrugged.

"Then, after we got away from the dog, he kept on blinking that dumb light at us," said the girl. She pointed to the roof of the Biggs' house. "It came from up there."

"That was my brother, Tom!" said Lucy pointing to Tom. "And he's not a dope! You could have been eaten by that dog. Tom saved you by shining the light in the dog's eyes so you could get away."

"Are you kidding?" said the girl. "We never need any help. We can take care of ourselves, right, Chip?" She turned to the boy standing beside her.

Chip nodded his head without saying anything.

"Anyway," Tom said. "I'm Tom Little and this is my sister, Lucy. We live in the walls of this house. Where are you from?"

"The city," the girl said. She pointed down the road.

"Wow!" said Tom. "That's at least *five* miles away. How did you get way out here? Are you lost?"

"Are you kidding?" said the girl. "We got *deserted*, that's what happened. Did you see the car that was parked by the side of the road—where the guy was changing a tire?"

"Yes, he's gone," said Tom.

"Well, we came in that car," the girl went on. "We sneaked a ride in it. And we got out of the car for just a minute to look around. Then the dumb dog chased us and we had to climb the tree. Then the guy left before we could climb down, the big jerk!"

Tom smiled. "Everyone you know seems to be stupid," he said.

"That's the first smart thing you've said," the girl told him.

Lucy's eyes narrowed. She looked angry.

The girl laughed. "Just kidding," she said.

"What's your name?" asked Tom.

"I'm Midge," said the girl. She gave the boy a slight shove. "This guy's my brother, Chip."

"Chip doesn't talk," said Tom.

"I do *so!*" said Chip.

"Do you mean to tell us," said Uncle Pete, his voice rising, "that you and your little brother just decided to sneak a ride in a car without telling your *parents*?!"

"Sure," said Midge. "Why not? It's no business of theirs what we do."

"That's ridiculous!" shouted Uncle Pete.

"Take it easy, Uncle Pete," said Mr. Little, Tom and Lucy's father.

"Yes, please keep your voice down, Uncle Pete," said Mrs. Little. "I'm trying to get Baby Betsy to sleep."

All the Littles were in the living room of their apartment inside the walls. They had just met Midge and Chip and had heard about their escapade. Mrs. Little was feeding Baby Betsy her noonday bottle. Uncle Pete was limping back and forth in front of the fireplace. (He had been wounded in the Mouse Invasion of '35 and had walked with a limp ever since.)

Uncle Nick, who was once a soldier in the Mouse Force Brigade, sat on a hassock near the fireplace looking closely at Midge. "Do you know the man in the car?" he asked.

"Oh, sure," Midge said. "He's the Old Geezer—the man who owns the house we live in."

"Well, at least that makes sense," said Uncle Nick. "You knew he was going to drive back to the city so you knew you could get home."

"Oh, we didn't care about that," said Midge. "We weren't going back that way."

Grandpa Little, who appeared to be napping on the couch, suddenly opened one eye. "Now *this* is getting interesting," he said. "What manner of transportation have you selected for your return trip?"

"Huh?" said Midge.

"For heaven's sake—speak plain English, Amos!" said Granny Little, who was sitting in her rocking chair. "The poor girl doesn't understand you."

"Grandpa wants to know how you were going to get back home," Tom explained to Midge.

"Fly!" said Chip. He held his arms out to his side like wings and wiggled them.

"Right," said Midge. "We were going to fly home on the back of one of the Old Geezer's pigeons."

"Pigeons!" said Tom, wide-eyed.

"Yeah," said Midge. "You see, this guy—the Old Geezer—has racing pigeons. He keeps them in coops in the attic of our house. He takes them in his car far away from their coops, but no matter where they are when he lets them go they race straight for home."

"You can't fly on the back of a pigeon!" said Uncle Pete.

Midge laughed. "We already done it before," she said.

Chip nodded his head.

"Did your *parents* let you do that?" asked Granny Little. She had stopped knitting and was staring open-mouthed at the two City Tinies.

"They don't care," said Midge. "It's no big deal."

"I don't believe that, Midge," said Mrs. Little. "I'm sure they wouldn't want you to do that. It's terribly dangerous. Dear me!"

"It's easy," said Midge. She pulled a loop of twine from the backpack she had on. "I just put this around the neck of a pigeon, and me and Chip sit on its back and hold tight. Then, when the Old Geezer lets the pigeons free—we fly home. There's nothing to it. It's not dangerous."

"Unless you fall," said Grandpa. "Then you'll fall, all right—straight down . . . fast!"

"Grandpa!" said Lucy, "Don't make jokes. They could get *killed*!"

"Hey!" said Midge. "You guys really *are* worried about us. How come?"

Mr. Little looked at everyone, scratched his head, and said, "Well, Midge—I, for one, believe you don't quite realize that you mustn't do really dangerous things like flying on pigeons unless you have a good reason to do it."

"But it's *fun* to fly," said Midge. "Right, Chip?"

Chip nodded his head up and down.

"Well, then, you're certainly going to enjoy going back to the city," said Mr. Little, "because you're going to fly there. We're going to ask Cousin Dinky to take you and Chip home in his glider. He'll be coming back from one of his trips soon."

"Who's Cousin Dinky?" asked Midge.

"Wait'll you meet him," Tom said. "He flies this neat blue-and-white glider."

"Cousin Dinky is a great adventurer," Lucy added. "He and his wife, Della, fly everyone's mail all over the Big Valley."

"Great!" said Midge. "Maybe this Cousin Dinky guy will let me fly the glider."

Mr. Little chuckled. "I don't think you're ready to fly a glider, Midge," he said. "It takes skill to do that, which you can only get by lots of practice. Dinky, himself, had a few crashes and got some scratches and bumps before he practiced enough to become a good pilot."

"Forget it!" said Midge. "I hate that *practice* stuff! That's the cool thing about flying on pigeons. You don't have to know anything. You just hop on and off you go. And you go *fast*! Zowie!!"

Grandpa snorted. "Instant gratification!" he said from the couch. "That's the trouble with you, Midge. You aren't willing to take the time and hard work and practice to learn how to do something correctly."

"Oh, Grandpa," said Mrs. Little. "Aren't you being too hard on Midge? She's only a child."

"Hey! He's right!" said Midge, looking around at all the Littles. "I want to have fun. Practicing isn't fun."

"Do you know what?" Tom said to Midge. "Maybe if you *watch* Cousin Dinky when he flies you home, you might learn a little about how he does it."

"Speaking of your home, Midge," said Mr. Little. "Do you know the address of the house you live in so that Cousin Dinky can find it when you get to the city?"

"I never paid no attention to that," said Midge. "I don't know where the Old Geezer lives."

"That's too bad," said Mr. Little. "What about the last name of the Old Ge—that is, the people you live with. Do you know their last name?"

"They're the Hites," Midge said. "We live in the walls of their house just like you do here."

"Good!" said Mr. Little. "We'll look them up in the phone book and get the address."

"But they don't have no phone," said Midge. "They had it taken out because it cost too much money."

"Midge, dear," said Granny Little. She put her knitting down, folded her hands, and looked serious. "I do wish you'd learn to say, 'They don't have a phone' instead of 'They don't have no phone.' "

Midge turned to Tom. "What'd she say that for?"

Tom grinned. He lowered his voice so Granny couldn't hear him. "Oh, Granny is always correcting our English," he said. "You know—there's a correct way and an incorrect way to say things. Granny worries about that a lot."

"What'd I say wrong?" asked Midge.

"You said, 'They don't have no phone.' "

"Well they *don't!*" said Midge. "That ain't wrong."

Grandpa Little suddenly sat bolt upright on the couch. "I've got it!" he said. "Why didn't I think of it right away?"

Everybody looked at the old man.

"I've been thinking about how to find out where Midge and Chip live," he explained, "and the answer is: Dinky should fly them to the city library and ask Carleton Booker."

"Who's he?" said Lucy.

"Oh, of course," said Mr. Little. "Carleton Booker."

"Good idea," said Uncle Nick.

"The historian of tiny people," said

Uncle Pete. "He'd know, wouldn't he?"

"For many years," said Grandpa Little, "Carleton has been writing his book about the many different kinds of tiny people and their family histories. He's sure to know where Midge's family lives."

"What is your last name, Midge?" asked Mr. Little.

"Scanty," said Midge. She nudged Chip with her elbow. "Me and Chip are Scantys."

"I think you mean to say, 'Chip and I,'" said Granny Little. And then she repeated it. "Chip and I are Scantys."

"You're kidding!" said Midge, laughing. "You ain't no Scanty."

"Tom and Lucy should go with Dinky and Della and the Scanty kids to visit the Booker family," Grandpa went on. "Surely Carleton knows where they live, and if he doesn't, he probably has the resources to find out. In any case, the children will enjoy meeting him. He's a most interesting person."

"Crimeny!" Midge whispered to Tom. "That sounds real boring—some old guy in a liberry with books and stuff."

"Don't you like stories?" Tom asked.

"Yeah," Midge said. "I *love* TV!"

"What about stories in books?" whispered Tom. "Don't you like them?"

"TV is lots better!" said Midge. "You don't have to read all those *words*! That's hard work."

"Can you . . . read, Midge?" said Tom in a low whisper.

"Sure I can read," replied Midge, looking shocked. "I'm not an idiot! I read the *TV Guide* all the time."

"What's your favorite book, Midge?" asked Lucy, getting in on the whispered conversation.

"*The Wizard of Oz*," said Midge. "Dorothy is the best—she sings real good!"

"*Midge!*" said Tom. "That's not in the book! It's only in the movie!"

All the grown-ups were leaning forward trying to hear what the children were
saying.

"Tom," said Mr. Little. "Would you
like to share with the rest of us what you
and the children are talking about?"

"It was books, Mr. L.," said Midge.
"We were talking about books."

Tom shrugged his shoulders and rolled
his eyes.

IT turned out that Cousin Dinky and Della weren't supposed to deliver the Littles' mail for a few days. Mrs. Little put the city children in a spare bedroom.

"Your parents are going to be terribly worried about you," said Mrs. Little, "but there's nothing we can do to tell them you're safe."

"Nobody's going to be worried about me and Chip," said Midge. "They know we can take care of ourselves."

"I wish I could believe that, Midge, dear," Mrs. Little said, "but I'm sure you're wrong. I know I'd be terribly upset if Tom and Lucy disappeared for a week."

The next morning when Tom and Lucy got up, they went to wake up the Scanty children.

They were gone from their room! And the place was a mess, with clothes, sheets, and blankets strewn around.

Tom and Lucy searched all the rooms of the apartment but Midge and Chip were nowhere to be seen.

When Mrs. Little heard the news she said, "Maybe they decided to go home by themselves. Midge is certainly bold enough to try and do it."

"That's terrible!" said Lucy.

"They'll get lost," said Tom.

"Before we decide that," said Mr. Little, "we need to search the wall passageways and look in the Biggs' rooms. We have to hurry. The Biggs will be up soon."

So, all the Littles except Granny and Grandpa Little headed for the tin-can elevator to get to the first floor of the Biggs' house. After they climbed aboard the tomato can for the trip down, they discovered the lifting strings were tangled and the elevator wouldn't move.

"Why, this is a mess," said Mr. Little. "It looks like we have a terrible tiny kid on our hands."

"What will she do next?" said Uncle Pete.

Uncle Nick volunteered to untangle the elevator strings. The rest of the Littles made their way to Henry Bigg's room (he was still asleep) where they found his pet parakeet flying about the room. The bird cage door was open.

"They've been here all right," said Mr. Little.

"Maybe Henry left the cage door open," Tom suggested.

"I doubt that, Tom," said Mr. Little. "Let's keep moving!"

Next, they went to the Biggs' kitchen where they found the honey-bear jar turned over on the counter. It was dripping honey.

Uncle Pete pointed to the counter. "Footprints," he said. "They've walked in the honey and tracked it all over."

Mrs. Little said she would stay behind and clean up the mess while the other Littles continued to search for Midge and Chip.

"Be very careful, Wilma," Mr. Little said. "I can hear the Biggs walking around upstairs. We're running out of time."

The Littles ran across the floor of the kitchen toward the living room. They heard Mr. Bigg's footsteps on the stairs.

At that point the Littles caught up with the runaway children. They were in the Biggs' living room sitting on a footstool and staring up at a large television that they had turned on by themselves.

"Get down from there immediately!" Mr. Little whispered fiercely.

"Shhhh!" said Midge. She motioned for everyone to keep quiet. "We're watching TV."

"*Mr. Bigg is coming!*" said Mr. Little as loudly as he dared. "Run for the radiator."

The Scanty children leapt off the footstool. They tumbled on the rug and ran under the radiator. The Littles were waiting for them near an opened secret door.

As everyone ran through the doorway they heard Mr. Bigg saying, "Now who in the world left the TV on all night long?"

Midge and Chip were hurried back to the Littles' apartment in the walls. While the rest of the Littles prepared breakfast, Mr. Little took Midge and Chip into the living room to talk to them.

"Midge," he said, "I don't want you and Chip to leave our apartment the rest of the time you are with us. We try not to go into the Biggs' rooms unless it is necessary. And, if we have to we are careful not to do anything that would show them we are here."

"We were just trying to have a little fun, Mr. Little," said Midge. "What do you do around here for fun anyway?"

"The first thing we do in the morning is to eat breakfast together," said Mr. Little, "and then we do our chores. Fun comes after chores."

"Chores?" said Midge. "What are chores?"

"Well, for instance," Mr. Little said, "the first chore you and Chip should do is to make your bed and straighten up your room."

"Is it crooked?" asked Midge, grinning slightly.

Mr. Little laughed. " 'Straighten up' means to clean up the room—make it neat," he said. "Pick up the pajamas we loaned you and hang them in the closet, make the bed—things like that."

Midge, still grinning, said, "I know what 'straighten up' means. I was only kidding."

"You have a good sense of humor, Midge," said Mr. Little.

"But, Mr. Little," Midge went on, "why should we bother making the bed? We're just going to mess it up again to-night."

"Just do it for me, Midge, please," said Mr. Little. "Mrs. Little and I like a neat and clean home. It would make us happy if you would help us to have one while you're here."

"Oh, okay, Mr. Little," said Midge. "It sounds silly to me, but me and Chip will do it if you want us to."

"Good," said Mr. Little. "Thank you."

"We never do chores where we live," said Midge. She turned to her brother. "Do we, Chip?"

Chip shook his head no.

"Do you mean that your parents do *all* the work?" Mr. Little asked.

"Naw! They don't do nothing either, not very much anyway."

Mr. Little chuckled. "Your home would be like a pigpen if that were true, Midge. But it's a good joke."

"No joke, Mr. L.," said Midge. "We all like the place to look a little piggy-pen-like. Say 'oink-oink,' Chip, if I'm right."

"Oink-oink!" said Chip.

"See?" said Midge. "Now that's a joke!"

"WELL," said Uncle Pete. He looked around, then whispered, "It's been quite an adventure so far, having the terrible tiny kid with us."

It was evening. The grown-up Littles were sitting in the living room talking after dinner. The children were playing a game in the kitchen. Uncle Pete was walking back and forth in front of the fireplace. "Midge is quite a character," he went on. "She's a tough little kid. Her parents must be a couple of . . . well, dillys! They haven't managed to teach her anything."

"That's hard to believe," said Mrs. Little. "Maybe Midge just doesn't want to learn."

"She'd be a problem for any mother and father to handle," said Granny Little.

"But . . . you know, I *like* her! She has spirit and energy. Anyone trying to bring her up would have to have energy and spirit themselves . . ."

". . . or she would eat them alive!" said Uncle Nick.

"*Eat* them?" said Mrs. Little.

"Well, drive them crazy at least," explained Uncle Nick.

"Oh, my goodness!" said Mrs. Little. "She's only a little girl, for heaven's sake."

"Here come the children now," said Mr. Little.

Lucy rushed into the room ahead of the others. "Daddy!" she yelled. "Midge says I'm a *wimp* because I like to read."

Midge was right behind her. "I never did!" she yelled. "I called her a *nerd*, not a wimp. It's nerds who read books, not wimps. Everybody knows that."

Tom and Chip brought up the rear. "These two girls argue all the time," Tom said. "They're driving me and Chip crazy, right, Chip?"

Chip nodded his head up and down.

"They're driving 'Chip and me' crazy," said Granny Little, correcting Tom. Then she turned to Midge. "What's the difference between 'nerp' and 'wimf'?"

"That's *nerd* and *wimp*, Granny," said Mr. Little. "All right, Midge—how come you think Lucy's a nerd and not a wimp? And what's the difference between those two words?"

"I know what a nerd is," said Chip suddenly. "A never-ending radical dude! N-E-R-D, get it?"

"Chip!" said Midge. "That's not it. A nerd—let's see," Midge began. "That's a guy who, you know . . . they're always trying to do the right thing. They never take chances and they wear—probably— glasses. I know Lucy doesn't wear them, but if she had to—she'd probably even *like* it."

Tom laughed. Lucy looked astonished. "I . . . I . . . " she stammered.

But Midge went right on. "The worst thing is, a nerd *likes* teachers. They sit in the first row like teachers' pets do, you know? And the worstest thing is they *like* to read books."

"And what's a wimp?" asked Lucy.

"Oh . . . a wimp," said Midge. "They're wishy-washy guys and you can beat 'em up easy. They're like Silly Putty. You know—they don't know what they think and they'll believe anything anyone tells them."

"Then you think I'm a nerd instead of a wimp?" Lucy asked.

"Yep!"

"Oh, good!" said Lucy.

"Wonderful," said Mr. Little. "The disagreement is over. Now I think it's time we got around to reading our story."

"Story? What story?" said Midge.

"We always have family reading time after dinner every other night," said Tom. "It's fun."

"You don't look at TV after dinner?" asked Midge.

"Not often," said Mr. Little. "If we want to look at TV we have to sneak a look at what the Biggs are watching. The only time we can look at something *we* want to see is when the Biggs are out of the house."

Lucy laughed. "And sometimes the Biggs come back before the program is finished, so we never know what happened at the end."

"That's only one of the reasons why we read books," said Mrs. Little.

Mr. Little smiled. "I guess you could say we're all nerds here, Midge. We like books."

"Why, when I was a girl there was no television," Granny Little said. "We always read books. And we were lucky because the people we lived with had lots of good books."

"But," said Midge, "there aren't any *pictures* when you read books."

"Some books are picture books," said Mr. Little, "but this month we are reading a storybook. There are no pictures at all. We just read the story and imagine the pictures ourselves."

"That's stupid!" said Midge. She sat down and folded her arms. "I'd rather look at TV."

"You can do that, Midge," said Mr. Little. "All you have to do is go down the wall passageway a short distance to where there are peepholes in the wall that faces the Biggs' television set. You can watch from there. The rest of us will be right here listening to a story."

Midge hopped out of her chair. "Great!" she said. "Come on, you guys. Let's go!" She started for the door.

Tom and Lucy stayed where they were. Chip got up slowly and walked after his sister. Then, he seemed to change his mind and went back and sat down.

"What's the matter with you guys?" yelled Midge. "Let's go! Maybe Henry

Bigg is looking at *Teenage Video Rescue Squad*." She looked at the watch over the mantelpiece. "It's on channel five right now. After that comes *Teenage Haircut Party*. It's super cool, man!"

Tom and Lucy didn't move. Chip shook his head no.

"C'mon back, Midge," said Tom.

"Sit down, Midge," said Granny Little. "We'll tell you what has happened in the story so far."

"Yes—come on back and listen," said Uncle Nick. "I think you—especially you, Midge—will be interested in the girl in the story."

"Give it a try, Midge," encouraged Uncle Pete. "I'll bet you'll like it."

"Great balls of fire," mumbled Grandpa Little. "Let's go—read the story. This discussion is making me sleepy. And when I sleep, I snore, and when I snore *no one* can hear anything! At least that's what Granny tells me."

Midge laughed. "Okay, Grandpa Little—I'll listen once," she said. "It'd better be good or I'll never do it again."

All the Littles clapped.

Chip shouted, "Hooray for my sister!"

Everyone looked at him.

"OOPS!" said Chip. He put a hand over his mouth. "I'm sorry."

Midge walked over and sat next to Chip. She nudged him in the ribs. "Little brother—you're a traitor," she said, and then, "So what's the big deal? I read a story once. What's it all about anyway?"

"WE are reading a story about one of the big people—a girl," said Mr. Little. "Her name is Gilly Hopkins. She's eleven years old and very intelligent, but she has problems."

Granny Little said, "She certainly does! Lots of problems."

"First of all," said Mr. Little, "Gilly is a foster child. That means that someone other than her parents has to provide a home for her."

"What happened to her parents?" asked Midge.

"At this point in the story nothing has been said about her father," said Mr. Little, "so he isn't taking care of her."

"Her mother isn't taking care of her either," said Lucy. She was sitting beside her mother, who reached over and took her hand.

"Where's her mother?" asked Midge. She had a pained look on her face. "She's dead, isn't she? I know this story. I don't like it."

"No, no, Midge—you must be thinking of another story," said Mr. Little. "Gilly's mother lives somewhere in California and Gilly lives in Maryland. When the story opens, she is on her way to live with her third foster mother in three years."

"What's her mother living in California for?" Midge asked. "Why doesn't she take care of her own kid?"

"Because she's a dope!" snapped Tom.

"Now, Tom—be fair. We don't know that," said Mr. Little. "We've only read a few chapters of the book and we don't know yet why Gilly's mother isn't taking care of her."

"She has to be dead," Midge insisted.

"All we know at this point about her mother is from a picture Gilly has of her,"

Mr. Little went on. "When Gilly is alone in her room she takes out the picture and looks at it."

"Gilly thinks her mother looks like a TV star," added Lucy.

"And," said Mr. Little, "in the corner of the picture her mother has written 'For my beautiful Galadriel'—that's Gilly's real name—'I will always love you.' "

"Phooey!" said Tom. "If she loved her she wouldn't leave her in a foster home."

"Maybe," said Midge, "her mother wants to come back to her but she can't. Maybe she's being held captive against her will."

Mr. Little went on. "As far as we know, Gilly was so young when she was separated from her mother she doesn't remember her."

"The mother's *got* to be held captive," said Midge. "I think there was a TV story like this. Yep, I remember: The beautiful mother was held captive by some outer space alien monsters."

"At the point in the story where we left off," said Mr. Little, "Gilly is being driven to her new foster home by Miss Ellis who asks her to act nicely so her new foster mother will like her."

Then, Mr. Little walked across the living room to where a regular-size book called *The Great Gilly Hopkins* lay on the floor (the Littles had borrowed the book from the Biggs' bookshelf). "Let me read this part to Midge so she can see what Gilly thinks about acting nicely." He riffled the large pages until he found what he wanted. "Here it is: Gilly thinks, *. . . but I am not nice. I am brilliant. I am famous across the entire county. Nobody wants to tangle with the great Galadriel Hopkins. I am too clever and too hard to manage. Gruesome Gilly they call me . . . here I come, Maime baby, ready or not.*"

"That's the foster mother's name," explained Lucy. "She's Mrs. Maime Trotter."

"Gilly is *weird*!" said Tom. "Why wouldn't she want a nice foster mother?" He shook his head.

"She wants her *own* mother," said Lucy. "I know I would."

"Does this story have a happy ending?" asked Midge.

"I never give away the ending," answered Mr. Little. He smiled. "What do you think, Midge? Would you like to listen and find out?"

Midge settled back in her chair. "Read, Mr. Little!" she said. "I think I know how it's all going to turn out: Her mother is going to escape from the space aliens and she and Gilly are going to live near Disneyland happily ever after. I just wish there were pictures, that's all."

"All right," said Mr. Little. "Now, if someone will just wake up Grandpa I'll begin."

Mr. Little continued to read *The Great Gilly Hopkins* on Tuesday and Thursday night that week. The Scanty children got very interested in the story, especially Midge. She said, "I think Gilly is a little like me except I never do any of those bad things she does."

"Of course not!" said Uncle Pete, pretending to be shocked.

"Midge, you *never* do anything bad," said Grandpa Little as he winked at Granny Little, who said, "Do you have something in your eye, Amos?"

On Saturday morning everyone was looking forward to hearing the end of the story when, suddenly, Cousin Dinky Little and Della flew in. They landed their twin gliders on the Biggs' roof.

Mr. Little told the two pilots that Midge and Chip needed help to get back to the city. He said the children usually flew on pigeons to get there, but that he had promised them a glider flight back instead. And he told them about Grandpa Little's idea—that the Library Tinies should be able to find out where Midge and Chip lived.

"They need to be taken back right away," said Mrs. Little. "Their parents must be terribly worried."

"Then we should all get into the gliders at once," said Cousin Dinky.

"Yes," said Della. "The wind is blowing southeast toward the city today, but it may change by tomorrow. We should leave now."

"Right," said Mr. Little. He turned to Midge and Chip. "All aboard, children—time to go home."

"Aw," said Midge. "Can't we stay one more day?"

"Yeah," Chip joined in. "Me and Tom are having *fun*. He's my pal."

"Tom and Lucy can fly with you if you like," said Mr. Little. "Is that okay, Dinky?"

"There's room," said Cousin Dinky.

"Good!" said Chip.

"Yeah, but . . ." said Midge.

"No *buts*, Midge," said Mr. Little. He pointed to the gliders. "Go!"

"But," Midge said. Then the words came rushing out. "We haven't heard the end of the *story!*"

"Get into the glider, Midge," said Mr. Little. "You'll have to hear the end of the story some other time. No more stalling: Your parents are waiting for you to come home."

"That's baloney!" said Midge under her breath as she walked toward Cousin Dinky's glider. "Let's go, Chip," she went on. "It's time to get back to the *real* world."

"I get to sit with Tom!" yelled Chip as he climbed into the backseat of Della's glider.

As soon as everybody had fastened their seat belts, Cousin Dinky and Della pulled in the fishhook anchors that were holding the gliders down. The aircraft began to roll down the steep slope of the roof, moving faster and faster. At the edge of the roof the two pilots raised their wing flaps; the gliders rose into the air. They zoomed out over the Biggs' yard. In a few moments they had skirted some trees at the edge of the yard and, under the skillful hands of the pilots, began to climb higher into the sky.

"Neat!" exclaimed Midge.

"Better than pigeons?" asked Cousin Dinky.

"Slower . . . lots slower," Midge answered.

"But safer—*lots* safer," said Cousin Dinky. "I'm in control of this flyer. It goes where *I* want to go."

"I'll bet I could train one of the Old Geezer's pigeons to fly where I want to go," said Midge.

"You'd have to spend a lot of time training a homing pigeon to fly somewhere other than home," said Cousin Dinky.

"And don't forget," said Lucy, who was sitting next to Midge, "you don't like to work hard learning anything. You said so yourself."

"Okay, Lucy!" said Midge. "I was only trying to be funny. I guess you didn't get it."

The two gliders sped on toward the city. About halfway there, Lucy pointed above them in the direction of the sun. "Look," she said. "There's a beautiful kite flying above us."

"Where?" said Cousin Dinky, squinting into the sun. "Tell me quickly."

"Up there—to the left," said Midge. "I see it. Wow! Isn't that awesome?" She looked down toward the ground. "Where's the guy who's flying it?"

Cousin Dinky searched the sky. "Where's the kite string, kids?" he said. "I need to know immediately."

"Why?" asked Midge.

"Because," said Cousin Dinky, "we might . . ." Suddenly the glider spun around in the air. ". . . *hit it!*"

"We've hit the string!" Midge shouted.

When the glider stopped spinning it began to bob around like a boat in rough water. "Something's damaged," said Cousin Dinky, who was struggling to fly the glider. It was going every whichway.

And then it began to fall.

"We're going to *crash!*" yelled Lucy.

ABOUT one hundred feet above the ground, Cousin Dinky managed to straighten out the glider. He looked desperately around. "Where's Della?" he yelled.

"Behind us," Midge said.

"She's coming fast," said Lucy.

Della's glider flew up alongside them. "What's wrong, Dinky?" she called out.

"I can't control the right wing," yelled Cousin Dinky.

"Hold it as steady as you can," Della shouted. Then she flew closer to Cousin Dinky's glider and, after a few attempts, she managed to get the tip of her left wing under his damaged wing to support it. Together the two pilots made a bumpy landing on the nearest rooftop.

"Wow!" said Midge. "That was *totally* awesome!! How'd she do that, Dinky?"

"Practice," said Lucy, quick as a wink.

"Get outta here!" Midge exclaimed. "Della's a *genius*, that's how."

"Not quite a genius, Midge," said Cousin Dinky. "But she's a very good flier and, lucky for us, she has a lot of . . . guts." Then he hopped out of his glider and ran to thank his wife.

"Where are we, Cousin Dinky?" asked Tom as everyone gathered together on the roof.

"I was so busy trying to fly, I never looked," said Cousin Dinky. He glanced around. "Let me see. . . ."

Just then, two tiny people—a man and a woman—came toward them from behind the chimney. They spoke together, "Hello there, Dinky and Della!"

"Who's that?" Della whispered to Cousin Dinky.

"I don't know," said Cousin Dinky

under his breath. He walked toward the couple. "I've never seen either of them before."

"This is an unexpected pleasure," said the man as he took off his hat and bowed grandly. He spoke with an English accent. "Welcome to our humble castle."

The woman curtsied. She was wearing a long, flowing dress. "We're so glad you popped in. It's been dreadfully boring since we last saw you," she said.

Suddenly Cousin Dinky laughed loudly. Then Della said, "Of course—it's the Dappers!" And she laughed, too.

The children stood near the gliders looking puzzled.

"Kids—come here!" called Cousin Dinky. "I want you to meet the Dappers—Dot and Dan. They're slightly crazy."

"We are not!" protested Dan Dapper. And then he pulled his hair off his head, tossed it into the air, caught it, and stuffed it into his pocket.

"Geez!" said Midge. "Hey—do that again."

At that, Dot Dapper took hold of her nose (which appeared quite long and crooked) and pulled part of it off her face and offered it to Chip. He immediately ran behind his sister and peeked out at the Dappers.

"Don't be afraid, Chip," said Della. "They're actors! The hair and nose are makeup—it's all make-believe."

"Aw, I knew that," said Chip. He stepped out from behind his sister. "I was only *pretending* to be scared."

"Oh," said Dan Dapper. "Then you're an actor, too."

"Me and Chip can act," said Midge, "but you're both *great* actors. I really thought you were kings and queens and stuff."

"Well," said Dot Dapper, "thanks for the compliment, but I'm mostly the play writer. Dan is the great actor around here. I call him Dramatizing Dan—he was talking like an actor when we first met."

"Ah, yes!" said Mr. Dapper who began to talk very fast. "I was known as Dramatizing Dan in those days—the most daring darling that ever dragged a dazed damsel out of a dreary dungeon dripping with dew, delivered her directly to her daddy who was dazzled, delighted, but despondent until I discovered the dopes that duped his daughter and defeated their dastardly doings directly."

"Do it again!" said Chip.

"Oh, wow!" said Tom. "That was neat!"

"Yeah," said Midge. "But what does it *mean*?"

"What it means," said Dot Dapper, "is that's how we met and fell in love! Only Dan has it all mixed up. *He* was the one lost. And it was a cave, not a dungeon. And the bad guys were friends of mine, not 'dopes.' We were exploring the cave and found him wandering around in there." She laughed. "I could see right away he was helpless so I saved his life by marrying him."

"For which I thank you," said Mr. Dapper, bowing low.

Mr. and Mrs. Dapper invited the children into their apartment in the walls of the house. They had tea and talked. Meanwhile, Cousin Dinky and Della stayed on the roof fixing his glider so they could continue their trip.

The four tiny children learned that the Dappers wrote plays, made scenery, and acted in plays. They were usually performed in various tiny persons' homes. Of course, this required a lot of traveling, which was done on the back of a dog owned by the big people who lived in the house. The dog—a long-haired collie—was their friend. Dan and Dot managed to stay hidden in the animal's fur as they traveled from place to place.

"It sounds like fun, Mr. Dapper," said Tom.

"Oh, it is," said Dan Dapper. "We have lots of fun, don't we, Dot?"

"Yes, except for one thing," said Dot Dapper. "It's hard to write a good play. You must do lots and lots of rewriting before it gets to be any good. It's as if the story is inside you and it just doesn't want to come out."

"I know!" said Lucy raising her hand. "It's like a baby being born. It doesn't want to come out either. My mother told me."

"I guess it could be something like that, Lucy," said Dot Dapper. "I can't say." She looked at her husband. "Dan

and I haven't been lucky enough to have any children . . . yet."

"Crimeny! That's awful!" said Midge. She looked around the room at all the stage scenery, colorful costumes, and props. "Any kid would *love* to live here . . . to be in plays and dress up all the time."

Mr. Dapper smiled. "Dot and I agree with you, Midge," he said. "We need more actors in the family so she can write plays with more people in them."

"Decidedly!" said Dot Dapper. "It's hard to write plays with only two characters. Sometimes I write a play with three or four characters, but since Dan and I are the only people acting, we have to run around like crazy changing costumes and makeup because only the two of us can be on the stage at the same time. It's not easy."

"But there's an *easy* way to fix that," said Midge. "Me and Chip can stay and help you. Both of us love to play make-believe. Honest."

"Oh, Midge, that would be wonderful but not now," said Mrs. Dapper. "Maybe someday you and Chip can come for a visit. In the meantime we understand you have been gone for a week and your parents are probably terribly worried about you."

"Oh, sure!" said Midge. "*Everybody* says that."

"Isn't it so?" asked Dan Dapper.

"If you say so, I suppose," said Midge.

"I think I'd like to write a play about

what is happening to you and Chip—your adventures," said Dot Dapper.

"But, no one knows the end of the play yet," said Lucy, "so how can you write it?"

"I could make it up," said Mrs. Dapper. "I do have an imagination. It should be a strong, believable ending, one that makes everyone feel that the story is over—really over."

"Well, geez—think of an ending!" said Midge. "Make it a happy ending—they're the best."

"I'll think about it, Midge," said Dot Dapper. "Maybe you should think about it, too."

"Hey," said Tom. "Maybe we could all be in the play. I think our parents would let us visit for a while."

The tiny people talked the rest of the day and into the late afternoon about getting together to produce a play. Finally, Cousin Dinky and Della came down from the roof and announced the glider was fixed and ready to fly again. By that time it was so late the Dappers invited everyone to stay overnight.

On the roof the next morning, Midge said, "Me and Chip are coming back. I promise!" She ran to Mrs. Dapper and hugged her. "And I *never* break my promises. I'll be back."

"Me, too!" yelled Chip as the gliders flew off toward the city.

"DINKY! Della! Welcome to the Tiny Peoples' Library," said a short, very old bald-headed man when the two gliders landed on the roof of the City Library Building.

The Littles and the Scanty children climbed out of their aircraft. They ran to greet old Mr. Carleton Booker who was coming through a small secret door on the roof of the building.

"Mr. Little called on the telephone last night to ask if you had gotten here," said Mr. Booker. (The tiny people know how to use the big people's telephones when they are asleep.) "He was worried when he learned you hadn't. I'll give him a call tonight."

Midge was standing apart from the others. She was looking at Carleton Booker with amazement. "Crimeny!" she said. "You're *old!*"

"I may be old," Mr. Booker shot back, "but I'm still kicking!" And then he kicked his foot back and forth several times.

Chip yelled, "Watch out, Midge!" Then he ran behind Cousin Dinky and peeked out.

"No fooling," said Midge. "I'm serious." She squinted at Mr. Booker, studying him. "You're the oldest person I've ever seen in my entire life."

"Midge, that's terrible!" said Cousin Dinky.

"That's really not too interesting, Midge," said Della.

"It is to *me*," said Midge.

"I know what!" said Chip, coming out from behind Cousin Dinky and jumping up and down. He pointed to Mr. Booker. "He's wearing *makeup* just like Mr. Dapper did."

Everybody laughed.

At that point Cousin Dinky introduced all the children to Carleton Booker who shook hands all around.

"Mr. Little told me why you've come," said Carleton Booker. "Let's get inside. I need some information from young Midge here if we're going to find out where these children live."

Mr. Booker took them through the secret door into a dark, dusty, and cobwebby room where there were thousands of books on shelves and in boxes and barrels.

"What a lot of books!" exclaimed Lucy

"This can't be the big people's *library*!" said Della.

Mr. Booker laughed. "No," he said. "That's down below on the next two floors." He waved his arms at all the books. "These are mystery books—detective stories, every one of them." He went on, "The rich old woman who lived in this mansion loved mysteries and it looks as though she owned every one that was ever published. When she died she left the building to the city to use as a library if they would use her books. Of course, the librarians couldn't use *all* the mystery books or there wouldn't have been room for anything else."

"I *love* mysteries," said Midge. "Me and Chip look at them on TV all the time."

A few minutes later they got to the Booker apartment inside the second-floor walls of the library reading room. Carleton Booker lined up his large family in a row. He went down the line tapping each person on the shoulder and saying their name, then giving each a number. ". . . she's number six and he's number seven," until he got to number eighteen, his wife, when he said, ". . . and this is Molly, my number-one helper."

The Booker family laughed loudly. "Whoops!" one said. "That's a good one!"

Mr. Booker pretended to look shocked. "Did I say something funny?" he asked.

"Grandmother is no one's *assistant*!" said one young woman.

"Oh, no?" Mr. Booker said. "What is she then?"

"She's the librarian!" said someone.

"What!" said Mr. Booker. He looked up and down the line. "Who said that?"

They all pointed to the smallest person.

"I beg your pardon, Emily," said Mr. Booker. "But if Mrs. Booker is the librarian, what am I? Chopped liver?"

Emily giggled. "No-o-o, Grandpa," said Emily. "You're the writer."

"Oh, sure—I'm the writer, all right," said Mr. Booker. "I'm also the librarian, and that's a fact, and Mrs. Booker is my helper: She's the *assistant* librarian."

All the Bookers began booing.

One man said, "Grandmother set up the filing system. She knows where *all* the books are."

"Didn't I give the orders to set it up?" said Mr. Booker.

"You did," said the man, "but, Grandpa—you couldn't actually *find* a book unless it fell off the shelf and landed in front of you. Isn't that the truth?"

Mr. Booker turned to his visitors and threw up his hands. "As you can see, I get very little respect in my own home." He turned to his wife. "Molly—tell these ungrateful relatives of mine that I'm the librarian."

"You're a wonderful writer, dear," said Mrs. Booker. "And also, you *believe* in the library. You started it, you're a great reader, and you've inspired all of us to read and learn."

"What's your favorite story for kids, Mr. B.?" said Midge.

"Well, Midge, my favorite storybook to read aloud to children is *Winnie the Pooh*," said Mr. Booker. "But when I was your age the book I loved the most was *Treasure Island*. I read it many times."

"When I'm not looking at the Saturday-morning cartoons, which *I* love the most," said Midge, "I guess my favorite book is *The Great Gilly Hopkins*, but I don't exactly know how it ends. You see, we were at the Littles' house and we had to leave in a hurry so I never got to know how it ended."

"Not to worry, Midge," said Mr. Booker. "We have a tiny person's copy in the library. Since you may be here for a while until we can find out where you live, you can check the book out of the library and finish reading it. Do you have a card?"

"A card?" said Midge.

Molly Booker said, "You'll need a library card to take a book out of the library, Midge—and, of course, you don't have one because you've never used our library. I'll get one ready for you to sign."

"Uh . . . well," Midge said. "Couldn't Mr. Booker read the book to all of us? Then I wouldn't need no . . . I mean *a* liberry card. Besides, I don't want to listen to no more . . . er, I mean *any* more books after this one anyway. It's just that . . . I'm interested in Gilly—know what I mean? I don't like *books*, I just want to find out what happened to her."

"Sorry, Midge," said Mr. Booker, "but I can't read the book to you at this time. I'm in the middle of reading *James and the Giant Peach* to everyone. You're invited to listen if you like."

Midge looked around at everybody. "Maybe one of you guys can tell me how it all turned out," she said.

No one said anything.

"Holy bananas! Nobody's going to help me," cried Midge. Then, "Is there one of them videocassette movies of the story? Does the big liberry have a VCR? Maybe I can look at it at night, right?"

"I've got an idea, Midge," said Emily holding up her hand.

Midge looked down at the little girl. She shrugged. "Okay, Emily—what's your big idea?"

"*I'll* read *The Great Gilly Hopkins* to you," said Emily.

AFTER everybody sat down to have lunch, Carleton Booker took Midge, Chip, and the Littles to his office.

"As you Littles may have heard from your grandfather, my good friend, Amos Little, I am writing a history of the tiny people of the Big Valley," Mr. Booker said. He paused to put on one of the two pairs of glasses that were hanging on ribbons around his neck. Then he began leafing through a book page by page. "I have studied the Tree Tinies, Trash Tinies, Ground Tinies, House Tinies, Brook Tinies, and the Hill Tinies so far—and, of course, I've studied my own people, the City Tinies."

"Wow!" said Tom softly.

"Surprisingly," Mr. Booker went on, "it has been easier to get information about people as far away as the Hill Tinies way up on top of Smoke Mountain than it has been to get correct information about the City Tinies right here in town."

"Why is that?" asked Cousin Dinky.

"It's because there are so many of them," replied Mr. Booker, "and, the long and short of it is, after going over and over my data, I'm sorry to report I have nothing on the Scantys."

"Oh, my!" said Della looking at Midge and Chip.

"Well," said Midge. "If you can't find where we live, may . . . be we'll have to live somewhere else."

"Let's live with the Littles or the Dappers!!" Chip shouted with a big grin on his face.

Mr. Booker paid no attention to the Scanty children. "Nary a clue did I find as to where they live," he said. "However, I have one last idea." As he walked to a

wall map on the other side of the room he took the first pair of glasses from his nose and put on the second pair. "Midge or even Chip may recognize or remember the name of the street they live on if they see it or hear it spoken."

So, for the next hour, the Scanty children watched and listened as everyone else took turns reading street names to them from the city wall map. Nothing sounded familiar to Midge and Chip.

"Hold it!" said Tom. "I think I just figured it out—holy cow, it's simple. Why didn't we think of it before now?"

Everyone turned to look at the tiny boy.

"Midge," said Tom, "when does the old guy . . . er geezer take his pigeons out in the car so they can fly home?"

"You remember, Tom," Midge answered. "It was Saturday we came to your house. He also flies his pigeons on Wednesdays and Thursdays."

"But, at what time of day?" Tom asked. "The same time?"

"Yeah," said the tiny girl. "It's noon, always twelve o'clock noon."

"That's right, Tom," said Lucy. "Remember? It was noon—Mirror-Message Time—when we tried to signal Tina Small."

"Then all we have to do," said Tom, "is be up in the air in the gliders sometime after twelve o'clock noon, and when the pigeons come flying by, we follow them to the Scantys' house."

"Tom—that's it!" yelled Cousin Dinky. "They'll take us straight there."

"It's a piece of cake," said Della. "On Wednesday, we'll get the gliders up in the air over the road that comes into town from the northwest. That's probably the way they'll be coming in; we can't miss them."

"You'll be staying here until the day after tomorrow," said Mr. Booker. "The children will have time to visit our library and see how we make our tiny peoples' books; they'll enjoy that. And, Midge will have enough time to hear the end of *The Great Gilly Hopkins*—that is, if she accepts Emily's offer to read it to her."

"Fat chance! I'm not going to let some little kid read a book to *me*!" said Midge. "No way! I don't *care* what the ending is. It's only a *book*! Books aren't real like television. You get to see the color and everything on TV—that makes it more realer."

"Of course, I don't think that way, Midge," said Mr. Booker. "Perhaps it's because when I was a child there was no TV, and movies were shown in theaters where tiny people didn't go. So, the first stories I heard were read to me from books and I've loved books ever since. They seem the most real to me."

"Books are better," said Lucy.

"Sure, Lucy," said Midge. "I *knew* you'd say that. You're just buttering up Mr. Booker 'cause you're a nerd."

"I like movies but books are better," said Lucy, "because you get to know the people in the story better."

"I believe that's because the story in a book sometimes tells what they're *thinking* about," Tom added.

"Oh, great!" said Midge. "That's all I need—two nerds!" She stomped out of the room.

THAT night the Booker family and the Littles got together to leave the wall apartment to go into the big library. Most of the Bookers went there to work. The Littles were going with them to see how they made books.

They walked through the dimly lit wall passageways.

"It's too bad that Midge is still angry," said Cousin Dinky.

"She locked herself in her room," said Tom. "I tried to tell her it would be fun to visit the big library, but she told me to 'get lost!'"

"*I* came, Tom," said Chip, tagging along behind Tom and pulling on his sleeve. "Hey, Tom—how come we're going to the big liberry at night?"

"You know, Chip," said Tom.

"Because there ain't no big people there at night. Right, Tom?"

"That's right, Chip—but don't say 'ain't,' say 'aren't.' "

"Aren't," said Chip to himself softly. "Is 'ain't' a dirty word, Tom?"

"No."

"Then how come I gotta say 'aren't' instead?" said Chip.

"Because 'ain't' is not the correct word, Chip—and 'aren't' is," Tom said.

It was dark when they entered the library through a secret door that led to a wide windowsill. A streetlight helped to light the room and to cast strange shadows from geranium plants in pots all along the sill.

The tiny people used the cords from the venetian blinds to lower themselves to a big open floor space several feet below the window. At this point the younger Bookers set about arranging books, sheets of paper, erasers, pencils, rulers, scissors,

and other necessary things on the floor. They brought them from every part of the library.

"Mr. Booker," said Cousin Dinky, "I've seen tiny people do marvelous things in this big world we live in, but nothing as fast or as well organized as this."

"Amazing!" said Della. "Everyone knows exactly what to do."

"We can thank Mrs. Booker for that," said Carleton Booker. "She's very interested in excellence and she has all the Bookers copying tiny peoples' books like a fine car maker makes cars: with quality controls and *fast*. The only part of the book making that goes slowly are the drawings and illustrations. Our artists create their own drawings back in our library, and that takes time."

"How do you choose which books to copy?" asked Della.

"Well," said Mr. Booker, "first, of course, we choose books children and adults like." Then he laughed heartily.

"And, second, we try very hard to get them from the two bottom shelves."

There was indeed a remarkable scene taking place in front of the Littles. Four books were being copied. Two of the Bookers held each book upright on the floor. A book was open to the page being copied, and the tiny person doing the copying knelt on a piece of typewriter paper in front of the book. Lines had been drawn across the paper and up and down on it—creating 121 small pages for a tiny book.

The back of the paper had lines drawn upon it in the same way. The odd page numbers of the tiny book were on one side of the paper, the even numbers on the other. Altogether there was room on one piece of paper—front and back—for 242 pages if they were needed.

After a page was copied, the two Bookers holding up the big book turned to the next page. One of them then held the book upright with the new page open while the other helped the person doing the copying flip the piece of typewriter paper over. The new page of the big book could be copied on that side. And so it went until the entire book was done.

"When we're through with copying the book," said Mr. Booker, "we take the piece of paper to the library copy machine and make five copies of it, front and back, using the thinnest paper we can find. Finally we cut out the pages and sew them together to make the finished book."

"But you are making five copies of each book," said Della. "Why do you want so many copies?"

"Because Molly Booker is on a *crusade*, that's why!" said Mr. Booker. "She calls it FETCH a Book! It means, 'For Every Tiny Child's Home—a Book.' You see, Molly has found out that many tiny children here in our city don't read well and she's determined to get books to them—good books. Some will be library books, of course; but she also wants to give away as many books as she can."

Cousin Dinky said, "I don't think we knew that so many children were not reading well."

"Oh, yes—it's a fact," said Mr. Booker. "Molly was helping me do research for my book and this is one of the things she learned. She's been working like a house afire on this problem ever since." The old man chuckled. "I can't get her to do any more research for me."

Cousin Dinky and Della looked at one another.

"Yes!" said Della, "I think we should." She nodded her head.

"I *knew* you'd agree with me," said Cousin Dinky.

"I beg your pardon," said Mr. Booker. "I'm afraid I don't understand what you two are talking about."

Tom said, "Oh, that's the way they are! Sometimes they talk to each other without talking. It's spooky."

"Dinky and I just decided we want to help in Mrs. Booker's FETCH a Book program," said Della.

"Della and I can distribute a lot of the books," Cousin Dinky went on. "We can fly around the city in our gliders dropping off books at tiny people's homes."

"We'll call it the Flying Bookmobile," said Della.

"Right!" said Cousin Dinky. "My thought exactly."

Just then Midge came sliding down the venetian blind cord. She rushed up to the tiny people, holding a book over her head. "Hey, you guys! Guess what!" she yelled. "I done it! I mean . . . I *did* it! I read the end of Gilly's story all by myself."

She was grinning widely as tears rolled down her cheeks.

WEDNESDAY at noon found the Littles
and the Scantys flying in the two gliders
above the city. They had said their good-
byes to the Bookers. Now they were
slowly circling in the sky hoping to see
the Old Geezer's pigeons coming toward
the city on their way home.

"Well, Midge—you and Chip should
be home soon," said Cousin Dinky.

"What's the big hurry, Dinky?" said
Midge. "Me and Chip are having fun.
Besides, I started reading another book."

"You should have checked it out of the
library," said Lucy. "Cousin Dinky and
Della could have picked it up on one of
the Flying Bookmobile's trips around the
city."

Midge pulled a book out from under
the seat. "Just kidding!" she said grinning.
"I got a liberry card and I checked it out
just before we left."

"Midge! You said . . ." cried Lucy.

Midge laughed. "I was just trying to
trick Dinky into going back," she said.
"We were having so much fun at the
Bookers, I didn't want to leave."

"Here they come!" shouted Cousin
Dinky, interrupting. He waved to Della,
Tom, and Chip in the other glider up
ahead.

For a few moments the pigeons seemed quite far away and moving slowly; but, suddenly, the birds were all around them flapping their wings. Then, they were gone!

The glider was left spinning around and pitching back and forth through the air like a small boat in a great ocean when a ship passes.

Cousin Dinky struggled to keep the glider under control. By the time he looked to see where the pigeons were, they were gone. "Did you see where they landed, kids?" he asked.

"I didn't see nothing!" said Midge. "I'm dizzy."

"It was like spinning on a swing," said Lucy.

"Hey, Dinky!" shouted Midge. "Where are Della and them?"

Cousin Dinky looked all around the sky. "Oh, no!" he said. "They're gone!"

Della's glider was nowhere to be seen.

"The only thing I can figure," said Cousin Dinky to Mr. Booker after they returned to the library, "is that Della's glider got damaged from those pigeons flying by, and she had to make an emergency landing."

"I certainly hope it's not any more serious than that," said Mr. Booker.

"We flew around for a long time after they disappeared, looking at rooftops and yards trying to find them," said Cousin Dinky.

"They weren't nowhere," added Midge.

"I wish Tom were here," said Lucy. "I miss him."

"They'll get back somehow, Lucy," said Cousin Dinky. "Della will find the way. In the meantime we'll keep busy. I want to put a propeller engine on the glider so we can keep up with those pigeons when they fly again tomorrow."

"Are we going to go even if they don't come back?" asked Midge.

"We *have* to, Midge. You and your brother have been away from home for too long," said Cousin Dinky. "I'm taking you back tomorrow whether they're here or not."

"But we should go look for them," said Lucy. There were tears in her eyes. "If *we* were gone they would look for us."

"At this moment," said Carleton Booker, "it would be like looking for a needle in a haystack. We should wait and have faith that Della can get them back. We need to give her a chance to do that."

By the next day at noon Della, Tom, and Chip were still missing. Cousin Dinky, who had rigged the glider with a rubber-band propeller engine, was determined to try to follow the homing pigeons again. Up on the library roof, the glider pilot called to Lucy and Midge to get aboard the aircraft. The two girls were saying good-bye to Mr. and Mrs. Booker.

"Now, Midge," said Mr. Booker, "you and Chip mustn't forget to keep in touch with us. We just know you're going to be great readers. You have a library card, so use it!"

"Remember," said Mrs. Booker, "Dinky will have his Flying Bookmobile operating soon. Once every few weeks he will visit you with new books and pick up the books you have."

The tiny girls hugged the two old people and then ran and climbed into the glider. In a few moments the blue-and-white craft was airborne and climbing into the sky.

"I have a plan," said Cousin Dinky. "They're not going to get away from us this time."

"What are you going to do, Dinky?" asked Midge.

"You just wait and see," said Cousin Dinky.

The tiny pilot glided along looking for a rising air current. When he felt a gentle upward push on the glider's wings he used it to climb higher into the sky. When he sensed the warm air was no longer lifting him, he searched for another rising current. Once in the current, he circled slowly so as not to glide out of it. Finally Cousin Dinky had positioned the glider high enough in the sky and at what he thought was the right place over the town. He looked around hoping to see the pigeons somewhere below and away from them racing toward their coops in the attic of the house where the Scantys lived.

"Lucy," said Cousin Dinky.

"Yes, Cousin Dinky," said Lucy.

"Keep looking for the pigeons while I talk to both of you," Cousin Dinky said. "Give a big yell when you see them."

"Yes, sir!" said Lucy. She shaded her eyes and peered toward the northeast, shifting her gaze as the glider circled in the rising air.

"Midge," said Cousin Dinky. "Are you ready?"

"Yessir, Captain Dinky!" Midge replied. She grinned and saluted with her left hand. Her right hand was holding a stick that came out of a hole in the floor of the cockpit she and Lucy were sitting in.

"This is my plan, girls," said Cousin Dinky. "We're go—"

"*Here they come!*" yelled Lucy as loudly as she could.

"Okay!" yelled Cousin Dinky. "No time for the plan. Just hold on to that stick, Midge, until I give the word to pull it out. First, we're going to dive in order to get going almost as fast as the pigeons."

"Go, Dinky! Go!" yelled Midge.

The tiny pilot was looking down over the side of the glider watching the approaching pigeons racing toward the city. Suddenly—when he decided the time was right—he slipped out of the rising warm-air current. Then he nosed the aircraft steeply toward the ground and began to dive. They were diving in the same direction the pigeons were flying in. Down they went, picking up speed, going faster and faster.

"*Zowie!!*" yelled Midge. "Right on, Dink! Right on!"

"Keep your hands on that stick, Midge!" shouted Cousin Dinky.

"Yessirree!" Midge yelled. "Holy cow, I love this!"

As the glider came out of its long, fast dive it was level with the pigeons but a good distance ahead of them. It was Cousin Dinky's plan to stay in front of the pigeons for as long as he could. He knew the pigeons were flying a lot faster than he was, but he was hoping to be close enough to them when they passed his glider to see them land at the Scantys' house.

"The pigeons are coming up fast!" shouted Lucy, who was looking back.

Cousin Dinky held his course. He glanced back. "Get ready with that stick, Midge," he said. "Don't pull it out until they pass us and I give the order, and do it only if we're still flying straight ahead. I'm going to try hard to keep us from flipping around like we did the last time."

And then the pigeons—one of the fastest-flying birds—were all around them in the sky flapping their wings and streaking past, wings humming, headed for their home loft. The air around the glider churned violently, tossing the aircraft like a dry leaf in a gale.

Cousin Dinky, using all his strength and flying skill, held the glider's nose straight and true. All too soon, however, the pigeons swept past. Then something happened that surprised Cousin Dinky— the glider was pulled forward rapidly in a swiftly moving air current that was created by the speeding pigeons. He rode the current expertly, and, looking ahead, saw that the pigeons were still in sight.

When the current that was pulling them along finally began to slow down, Cousin Dinky shouted, "Okay, Midge! Pull out the stick!"

Midge gave the stick a yank. It didn't move. Quick as a cat, Lucy grabbed hold of the stick and, together, the two tiny girls pulled it out of the hole in the floor.

The blue-and-white aircraft shot forward as the rubber band under the floorboards started to unwind and the propeller began to spin.

"Hooray!" yelled Midge and Lucy.

"Look, girls!" said Cousin Dinky a few moments later. He was pointing into the distance. "You can see the pigeons landing. We've found Midge's home."

"Oh, heck," said Midge. "It's all over. I wanted it to last forever."

Cousin Dinky headed the glider toward the house where the last of the pigeons were flying through the attic window into their home loft.

"Look, kids! There are tiny people standing on the roof waving at us." Cousin Dinky swooped down toward the house.

"It's *them!*" shouted Lucy. "It's Della

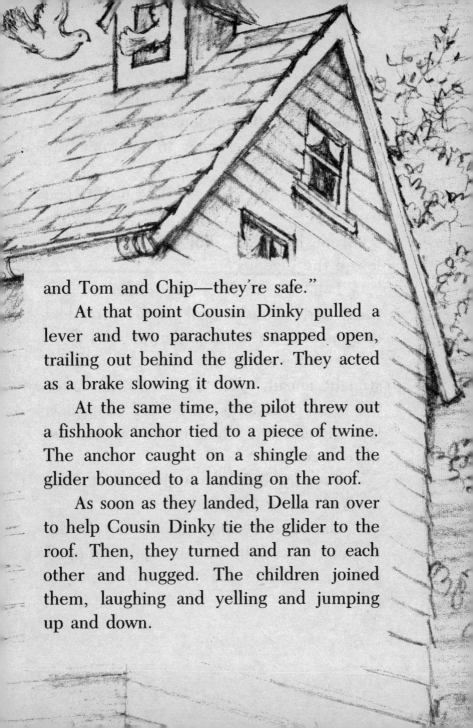

and Tom and Chip—they're safe."

At that point Cousin Dinky pulled a lever and two parachutes snapped open, trailing out behind the glider. They acted as a brake slowing it down.

At the same time, the pilot threw out a fishhook anchor tied to a piece of twine. The anchor caught on a shingle and the glider bounced to a landing on the roof.

As soon as they landed, Della ran over to help Cousin Dinky tie the glider to the roof. Then, they turned and ran to each other and hugged. The children joined them, laughing and yelling and jumping up and down.

"What *happened* to you?" said Cousin Dinky to his wife. "We thought you crashed when the pigeons flew by so fast. I figured you were trying to find your way back to the library."

"Tom," said Lucy. "I thought you were lost."

Tom laughed. "Not us—we just followed the pigeons."

"I lost control of my glider in the rough air," Cousin Dinky said. "You had disappeared when we pulled out of it."

"I managed to keep my glider facing straight ahead," said Della. "Then, after the birds passed we got sucked along in a fast current and when it died down, we were here."

"So why didn't you fly back to the library?" asked Cousin Dinky.

"Damaged landing gear," said Della. "I think a bird hit it. We almost flipped over in the landing. I've been trying to fix it."

The children ran over to Della's glider to look at the damage. This gave Cousin Dinky and Della a chance to talk alone.

"I suppose you've met Midge and Chip's parents?" asked Cousin Dinky.

"I've been in the apartment the kids live in," said Della. "And they don't live with their parents. It's their grand-parents—and they aren't young grand-parents."

"Where are the parents?" asked Cousin Dinky.

"They're dead, Dinky. It's very sad," said Della. "They died a few years ago in a fire. The aged grandparents are trying to bring them up—they really love the kids—but Midge and Chip are out of control. The place is a mess. The grand-parents are frantic. They just don't have the energy that's needed to bring up small children. So you can see, Midge is not a terrible tiny kid really. She needs closer care. She's really a good kid."

"Are you thinking what I'm thinking?" asked Cousin Dinky.

"Of course I am!" said Della. "We can help."

Cousin Dinky smiled. "Then let's tell Midge and Chip," he said.

So, hand in hand, the two tiny adventurers walked across the roof to tell the Scanty children their idea. If it was all right with their grandparents (and it was) Cousin Dinky and Della would drop in often to see the family and help in any way they could around the apartment. They promised to see to it that Midge and Chip would occasionally make flying visits to the Dappers, the Bookers, and, of course, the Littles.

And, later, after meeting and visiting with Grandmother and Grandfather Scanty, the Littles went to the roof, repaired Della's glider, and flew home.

AFTERWORD

TRUE to their promise, Dinky and Della saw to it that Midge and Chip visited the Dappers often. Dot Dapper wrote a play about them. Midge and Chip painted sets, acted, and traveled around the Big Valley putting the play on in tiny people's homes. Eventually they came to spend more time with Dot and Dan than they did with their grandparents.

Cousin Dinky was so pleased with the adventure that he wrote a song about it. It took him quite a long time to find an audience that was willing to sit still and listen to him sing the song (he sang off-key). Finally, Granny Little, who was hard of hearing, and Tom, who admired him hugely (but still sneaked cotton into his ears), and Della, who loved him, sat down to listen.

The intrepid adventurer strummed his guitar (which was out of tune because *he* tuned it) and sang this song:

Two stowaway kids in a pigeon crate
got chased up a tree 'til it got so late
they couldn't get down to go back home
the way they did whenever they roamed
on a pigeon.
On a pigeon?
On a pigeon.
On a pigeon's back with a piece of string
these tiny kids did the scariest thing.
Just a couple of Scantys named Midge and Chip
on any old noon they'd take a trip.
On a pigeon.
Nestled in the feathers
of a big gray bird
The whistling wind
was all they heard.
Loved the ride and the excitement,
not forgetting what hold-on-tight meant
on a pigeon.
But this time . . .
The two tiny kids are really stranded.
No one knew where the pigeons landed.

Up to the Littles' home to ponder
what to do with kids who wander
far from home . . . yes, on a pigeon.
Came Dinky to the rescue with his glider.
In climbed Lucy with Midge beside her,
with Della taking both Tom and Chip
the gliders set off on a city-bound trip.
On a pigeon?
No—in gliders, silly!
Adventures in a library and with some actors.
Brand-new friends called Bookers and Dappers.
A near disaster with a kite string, too—
brave Della knew just what to do.
With a kite string?
No, a plane wing.
Following birds so incredibly fast
the pilots managed to land at last
on the Geezer's rooftop in the city.
Never did home look quite so pretty
with pigeons
on a rooftop
in the city!

Uncle Pete, who had found an excuse not to listen, said, "I'm so glad I wasn't there."

Look for other books about the Littles